# The Littlest Polar Bear

By Peter Strzyz

Published by Mindstir Media

1931 Woodbury Ave. #182 | Portsmouth, New Hampshire 03801 | USA

1.800.767.0531 | www.mindstirmedia.com


Printed in the United States of America

ISBN-13: 978-0-9908137-9-8

Library of Congress Control Number: 2015904941

# Dedication

To my nieces and nephew: Kiera, Gabriela, and Casey…
BE STRONG LIKE A POLAR BEAR!!

MINDSTIR MEDIA

This is Athena, the littlest polar bear in her celebration near a sea in northern Alaska.  Although she is small, she is strong and confident.

Athena loves adventures and exploring her playground of icy glaciers, blue seas, and towering mountains.

Her mom, Ursa, and dad, Ursus, always tell her to be careful. "Athena, it could be dangerous out there," said Ursus. "We don't want you to get hurt."

"Ehhkk! Mommy, Daddy... I'm not afraid of anything," Athena exclaimed.

Athena also loves to have snowball fights with her friends.

"We can't tell who wins because we all have white fur!" shouted the littlest polar bear.

One day, Athena goes out and notices the glaciers around her are melting because it is getting too warm, slowly taking away her home and food.  She becomes very worried.

"Umm… what's going on here?" Athena shrieked.  "I don't have as much room to play and explore anymore!"

Athena shows her parents that the glaciers are slowly disappearing.

"There's not enough room for all of us polar bears!" Ursus roared.

Athena's parents decide to leave northern Alaska and set off on a journey for a new home.

"I'll really miss my friends, but I can't be without my mommy and daddy," cried Athena.

So Athena and her parents start their journey through Alaska, when they come upon a very angry blizzard near the city of Fairbanks. They find a giant snow cave and make it their new home.

While the storm rages on, Athena wants to play in the snow but her dad is concerned about the bad weather.

"Athena, it's not safe out there for you because your mom and I can't see you in the heavy snow," implored Ursus. "Stay in the cave until the storm calms down and then you can go out and play."

The storm clears and Athena decides it's time to play. She meets Snickers, a black-and-white-spotted dog with only three legs.

"Hi! I'm Athena. I'm the littlest polar bear in Alaska," Athena introduced. "What's your name?"

"My name is Snickers!" pronounced the black-and-white-spotted dog. "I love to run, jump, and chase snowballs! Will you play with me?"

"Are you sure you can? You only have three legs," remarked Athena.

"Of course I can! My legs are so strong I only need three – and I can do anything I put my mind to!" Snickers boasted.

Right there, Athena – the littlest polar bear – realized she had a brave new friend named Snickers.

# GLOSSARY:

**Alaska:** The 49th state of the U.S.; largest state in the U.S. by area.

**Blizzard:** A snowstorm with strong winds that cause the snow to blow around which then makes it very hard to see.

**Celebration:** A group of polar bears.

**Fairbanks:** The second largest city in Alaska; population of 32,070 people (2012 estimate)

**Glacier:** A big sheet of ice on a mountain that moves very slowly.

**Ursa:** A group of stars that form a bear; Ursa Major forms the Big Dipper and Ursa Minor forms the Little Dipper.

**Ursus:** Latin for bear.

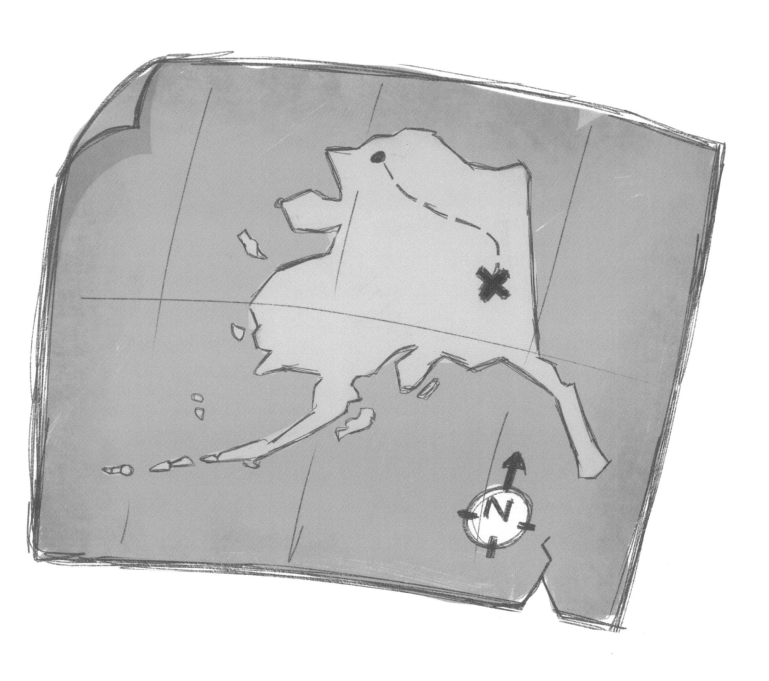

CPSIA information can be obtained at www.ICGtesting.com
Printed in the USA
BVIW12n1451010715
406948BV00012B/83